I Go with My Family to Grandma's

by RIKI LEVINSON • illustrated by DIANE GOODE

A PUFFIN UNICORN

Text copyright © 1986 by Riki Friedberg Levinson
Illustrations copyright © 1986 by Diane Goode
All rights reserved.
Unicorn is a registered trademark of Dutton Children's Books
Library of Congress number 86-4490
ISBN 0-14-054762-2
Published in the United States by Dutton Children's Books
a division of Penguin Books USA Inc.
Editor: Ann Durell   Designer: Riki Levinson
Printed in Hong Kong by South China Printing Co.
First Unicorn Edition 1990
10 9 8 7 6 5 4

to my warm and loving,
full-of-fun family—every one of you
R.L.

to Peter Goode
D.G.

My name is Millie
and I live in Manhattan.

I go with my family on a red and yellow bicycle

to Grandma's.

My name is Bella
and I live in Brooklyn.

I go with my family on a golden yellow trolley

to Grandma's.

My name is Carrie
and I live in Queens.

I go with my family in Papa's white wagon

to Grandma's.

My name is Beatie
and I live in the Bronx.

I go with my family on a dark blue train

and a dark green train

to Grandma's.

My name is Stella
and I live on Staten Island.

I go with my family in Papa's big car
on a red and white ferry

across the water, to the city

to Grandma's.

OUR FAMILY

CARRIE BEATIE STELLA MILLIE
BELLA